2015 July 14

Bear
and
Duck

Written and Illustrated by
KATY HUDSON

HARPER
An Imprint of HarperCollinsPublishers

Bear and Duck

Copyright © 2015 by Katy Hudson

For information address HarperCollins Children's Books, a division of HarperCollins Publishers,
195 Broadway, New York, NY 10007.
www.harpercollinschildrens.com

Library of Congress Cataloging-in-Publication Data

Hudson, Katy, author, illustrator.

Bear and Duck / written and illustrated by Katy Hudson. — First edition.

pages cm

Summary: "Bear doesn't want to be a bear anymore, so he tries out what it's like to be a duck. With a
few lessons from Duck, Bear realizes he makes a much better bear after all"— Provided by publisher.

ISBN 978-0-06-232051-3 (hardcover)

[1. Bears—Fiction. 2. Ducks—Fiction. 3. Self-acceptance—Fiction.] I. Title.

PZ7.H86653Be 2015   2013043137

[E]—dc23   CIP

                                                                                                                            AC

The artist used ink and watercolor to create the illustrations for this book.

Typography by Jeanne L. Hogle

15 16 17 18 19 SCP 10 9 8 7 6 5 4 3 2 1

First Edition

For my very special parents

QUACK!

Bear was a bear. And in most ways he was just like any other bear. He was big and furry. He slept all winter. And he ate lots and lots of honey. But in one big way Bear was not like other bears.

Bear's problem was that he wished he weren't a bear at all.

He was tired of sleeping all winter.
His fur felt hot in the summer.
And he was sick of all the angry bees.

"Leave. Me. ALONE!"

he growled, rubbing his sore,
stung nose.
  "That's it!" Bear decided.
"I am done being a bear."

Just then, Bear heard a noise. A happy, I-don't-sleep-all-winter-or-have-hot-fur-or-bees-stinging-my-nose kind of noise.

The sound was music to his ears.

So Bear slipped into the line
of happy yellow ducks.

QUACK!
He chimed in.

He watched the ducks' every move.

Yes! He could get used to being a duck. In fact,
he decided, he was a good duck!
Luckily, no one noticed the new duck. Until
Bear let out a too-loud and happy . . .

QUACK!

"STOP RIGHT THERE, BEAR! What are you doing in our line?" snapped Duck.

"You don't belong here."

"But please," said Bear. "I don't want to be a bear anymore. Can you please teach me how to be a duck?

PLEEEAAASE!"

"Well, all right," said Duck. "I guess I can help."

HOW TO BE A DUCK: RULE 1
NEST BUILDING

STEP 1:

Collect twigs and old leaves.

STEP 2:

Build nest.

STEP 3:

Place egg in nest.
Sit on egg.
Keep egg safe and warm.

STEP 4:

*Under no circumstances
should you lose your egg.*

HOW TO BE A DUCK: RULE 2
SWIMMING

STEP 1:

Waddle into water.

STEP 2:

Flap feet one at a time to swim.

STEP 3:

NO SPLASHING PERMITTED!

HOW TO BE A DUCK: RULE 3
FLYING

STEP 1:

Find perfect hill for takeoff.

STEP 2:

Run while flapping wings and keeping beak pointed upward.

STEP 3:

Once in the air . . .

CRASH!

"Oh dear."

This was definitely not going as planned.
Bear wasn't good at being a duck after all.

Duck felt sorry for Bear.
"Don't be sad, Bear. Look, you climbed a tree! Ducks can't do that!"

Bear felt a little better.
He decided to climb up and get that apple for Duck.

The apple was very high . . .
and the branch was very
bendy. . . .

Bear reached as far as he could, when . . .

BOOOIINNG!

"I'M FLYING!" Bear called out happily. "Just like a duck!"

But inside, Bear wasn't actually happy at all.

Flying twisted his tummy.

And the landing was far too tricky.

CRASH!

"I think I prefer climbing," he told Duck.

"Being a bear doesn't seem all that bad," said Duck.

"And you make a really good bear . . .

. . . and a really good friend."